For her love of birds and animals, infectious laugh, adventurous spirit, and boundless courage:

F O R   L Y N N

THE LITTLE
TOY SHOP

Written and Illustrated by

FRANCES WOLFE

TUNDRA BOOKS

Published in Canada by Tundra Books,
75 Sherbourne Street, Toronto, Ontario M5A 2P9

Published in the United States by Tundra Books of Northern New York,
P.O. Box 1030, Plattsburgh, New York 12901

Library of Congress Control Number: 2007938537

Library and Archives Canada Cataloguing in Publication

Wolfe, Frances
The little toy shop / Frances Wolfe.

Target audience: For ages 3-6.
ISBN 978-0-88776-865-1

I. Title.

PS8595.O588L48 2008   jC813'.6   C2007-906095-1

We acknowledge the financial support of the Government of Canada through
the Book Publishing Industry Development Program (BPIDP) and that of the
Government of Ontario through the Ontario Media Development Corporation's
Ontario Book Initiative.

We further acknowledge the support of the Canada Council for the Arts and the
Ontario Arts Council for our publishing program.

ONTARIO ARTS COUNCIL
CONSEIL DES ARTS DE L'ONTARIO

Medium: oil on Masonite

Printed in China

1 2 3 4 5 6   13 12 11 10 09 08

Once, when I was very young, I heard the story of a special little toy shop. It stood on a sunny street, right across from a park with whispering trees and a babbling brook. The shop was owned by Mr. Kringle, and his name was printed on the window in big gold letters.

Mr. Kringle was a gentle man, with rosy cheeks and hair as white as snow. He loved his little shop and all of the toys in it. But what he loved most was helping each and every customer find just the right toy.

One morning, a box was delivered to the shop. When Mr. Kringle looked inside, he found a small stuffed bunny, no more than eight inches tall. "Ho, ho, ho!" he chuckled. "What a cute little bunny."

Mr. Kringle put a price tag of five dollars on the bunny's foot. "I know just the spot for you," he said, placing him on a shelf next to a large teddy bear. "There, Teddy will look after you until I find just the right home for a cute little bunny like you."

That evening, Mr. Kringle put on his hat and coat and left the shop.

As the bunny sat quietly in the glow of the night-light, he heard a voice: "Welcome to the toy shop, little one!" It came from the bear sitting beside him.

"Why, thank you!" said the bunny.

Teddy introduced the bunny to all the other toys. He explained that each and every one was waiting for Mr. Kringle to find just the right child to take them home. "There is nothing sadder than a toy that never knows the love of a child," said Teddy.

As the days passed, Bunny and Teddy became the best of friends. Beyond their furry feet, they watched the world outside the shop change. Summer turned to autumn, and then came the cold white days of winter.

"Soon it will be Christmas," Teddy told Bunny. "It is a magical time, when many toys find loving homes."

As Christmas drew closer, the two friends saw more and more of the other toys leave the shop. They began to think that Mr. Kringle would never find just the right child for them.

One afternoon, a little girl appeared outside the shop. With cupped hands, she peered through the front window. Bunny was sure that she was looking right at him and his heart jumped with excitement. *Maybe this is the child who will love me,* he thought.

The little girl stayed there for a long time. She smiled and waved at him, but eventually she went away. Bunny was so disappointed.

To his surprise, she returned the next day and came into the shop.

"Would you like to hold him?" Mr. Kringle asked.

"Yes!" the little girl answered, beaming. He placed Bunny in her hands.

As soon as she touched him, Bunny felt all warm and tingly. In that instant, he knew that this was the child who would love him forever.

"I have only one dollar to spend," she said.

Mr. Kringle could see that this was just the right toy for her. "Well," he said, "as it happens, this bunny is on sale for one dollar." The little girl smiled. She told Mr. Kringle that she would come by with the money the next day.

That evening, Bunny and Teddy said their good-byes, for they knew that this would be their last night together in the toy shop.

On the gift tag: *To: The Birthday Girl* / *From: Dad*

The next morning, as Bunny was waiting for the little girl to arrive, a tall man and his assistant entered the toy shop. The tall man said, "I want to buy lots of toys; it's my daughter's birthday."

"How special to have a birthday so close to Christmas," Mr. Kringle said. "Now, what kind of toys does your daughter like?"

"I don't know," the man said, passing a wad of money to Mr. Kringle. "I'm sure this will cover any cost."

"But surely you want to get just the right toy for her?" Mr. Kringle protested.

As they spoke, the man's assistant scurried about the shop, stuffing toys of every description into a large brown sack. It wasn't until they had left that Mr. Kringle noticed that the bunny was gone.

That afternoon, the little girl came to take Bunny home.

Mr. Kringle explained what had happened and told her that the bunny was gone. "I'm so very sorry!" he said.

The little girl didn't say a thing. Tears pooled in her eyes. A great big one rolled down her cheek and fell to the floor with a *plop*.

The sound of it nearly broke Mr. Kringle's heart. Never before had a child shed a tear in his shop. He felt so badly that he offered her any toy in the shop for free.

$\mathcal{M}$eanwhile, the next thing Bunny knew, he was being stuffed into a box. Everything went black. Soon the box began to shake. He heard paper ripping and suddenly the top was pulled off. Looking up, he saw the birthday girl. She reached into the box and picked him up by his ear. He didn't feel all warm and tingly this time. Instead, he felt frightened.

As Bunny dangled in the air, the girl announced: "What a puny bunny. I don't want this silly thing!" She tossed him into a pile of torn boxes and crumpled paper.

Then, without a thought, she moved on to the next package.

$\mathcal{P}$oor Bunny – his day had started out with such promise. Now he found himself among the trash. The ungrateful birthday girl had broken many of the toys she'd been given. *At least I still have my arms and legs,* he thought, something that couldn't be said for some of the other toys.

As he lay there in the cold, a big dog came by. He sniffed at the bunny, then picked him up and trotted off, with Bunny dangling from his mouth.

After a while, the dog stopped and lay down. He placed the bunny between his paws to lick him. Then he started to chew. In no time flat, he had plucked one of Bunny's eyes right off his face.

The dog soon got up and trotted off again. This time, he dropped Bunny at the edge of the brook and began to drink. As he did, the babbling brook carried Bunny away.

He floated along – gently at first, but as the current grew stronger, he was tumbled and tossed on the dark ribbon of water. Suddenly his foot snagged on an overhanging branch. Bunny was stuck.

Mr. Kringle ran across the bridge. He slid down the snowy embankment to the water's edge. Careful not to fall in, he plucked the bunny from the icy brook.

Bunny felt warm hands squeezing the water from his fur. A familiar voice said, "My, my, little one, how did you ever end up like this?"

As soon as Bunny heard the voice, he knew it was Mr. Kringle, and a flicker of hope welled up inside him.

Mr. Kringle tucked the bunny into his coat pocket and, with a new spring in his step, he hurried home.

Mr. Kringle washed Bunny in a basin of warm sudsy water and dried him with a fluffy pink towel. "Now," he said, "let's see what we can do about that eye of yours." He took a needle and thread and sewed on a button where the bunny's eye used to be. "There now, you're almost as good as new."

The next day was Christmas Eve. Mr. Kringle took Bunny back to the toy shop. Bunny was looking forward to seeing his old friend Teddy again. But when he looked at their place on the shelf, Teddy was gone.

To Bunny's great surprise, Mr. Kringle appeared wearing a beautiful red-velvet suit trimmed with white fur. He was carrying a large sack filled with packages wrapped in brightly colored paper. Placing Bunny in a box, he said, "I know someone who will be very happy to see you!"

After a while, Bunny began to hear noises – jingling bells, swishing sounds, and then a great thump. The last thing he heard was Mr. Kringle as he whispered, "Merry Christmas, little one!"

For a long time, everything was quiet. Then Bunny heard a strange voice say: "Open this one. It's from Santa!"

When the lid was lifted off the box, Bunny could barely believe his eye. There was the smiling face of the little girl from the toy shop. His heart jumped for joy.

"It's my bunny!" she shouted, reaching into the box and picking him up. "I never thought I'd see him again." She gave Bunny a big hug and he felt all warm and tingly.

Bunny was so happy. The little girl didn't seem to care that his eye was missing, or that his fur wasn't quite as fluffy as it used to be. She loved him anyway, just the way he was.

That night, when the little girl went off to bed, Bunny got another big surprise.

There, lying on her bed, was his old friend. Bunny and Teddy had been given the greatest gift of all – a little girl with a heart big enough to hold them both.

On
a
sunny
street,
right across
from a park with
whispering trees
and a babbling brook,
there is magic to be found
in a little toy shop, where you
will
always
find just the right toy!